Amanda's
Secret
A Colonial Girl's Story

Jami Borek

Amanda's Secret

ISBN-10: 0991536614
ISBN-13: 978-0-9915366-1-0

Published by:

Shrewsbury
Press

chapter 1

Looking back, you could tell that it was bound to happen, though no one knew it at the time. As soon as Jane arrived at the Lambertson's plantation, Amanda's life was bound to change. The only question was, would it be a change for the better or (as it would be, if Jane had her way) a change for the very much worse?

It all started January sixth, the twelfth day after Christmas. Amanda had turned twelve just a few weeks ago, and she was going to her very first ball. She was excited for the company as much as for the dancing. It was pretty lonely, living on a large Virginia plantation and being the only child. She had no close friends to speak of, no one she knew really well. She was the kind of girl who could make friends easily, but she hardly ever had the opportunity to go to the neighboring plantations or to Williamsburg, the closest town. Everyone was always so busy, there was no one to take her, and she hadn't been allowed to go off visiting on her own. Her father was a lawyer, so when he wasn't at his office in Williamsburg, he was usually working in his study. Her mother was always busy too, running the plantation, and the servants of course had their own work to do.

So Amanda was very lonely, but she wasn't bored. She always had something to occupy her time. Most of the day she studied, with her mother's help or on her own. She practiced her reading and writing and sums, learned French and how to dance. She played the piano forte pretty well by now, and there was always her needlework when all else failed. She was still practicing fancy embroidery, but her plain sewing was already very fine. She'd made a shift for herself and a shirt for her father, and just yesterday she'd finished making her doll a ball gown with leftover bits of fabric from her own new gown.

Her new ball gown! It was thrilling just to think of it. It was yards of shimmering green silk, with a petticoat

It was the most beautiful
gown she'd ever owned

and a matching over-gown. The gown had a tight-fitting bodice trimmed with lace at the neckline, and the sleeves were trimmed at the end with flounces of lace. It had full, long skirts but was open at the front from the waist on down, so the richly ruffled petticoat could be seen beneath.

It was the most beautiful gown she'd ever owned. And this evening, this very evening, she would be wearing it out dancing, at her very first Twelfth Night ball. She was so excited, she could barely stand the waiting, and she woke up even before the dawn.

She lay in her four-poster bed in the velvet darkness, imagining how fine it all would be. The carriage ride through the silvery moon-lit forest would be magical—the moon would be full, the sky would be clear, and the ground would be covered with fresh new snow. After traveling through the forest and fields, she would finally see Mr. and Mrs. Hunt's house where the ball would be held. It would shine like a beacon in the darkness, brightly lit with candles in every room.

The coachman would help her down from the carriage and up the steps to the house. Then a footman would open the door and whisk away her warm wool cloak. The ballroom would be full of music, candle-light, and laughter. It would have blazing fires in every fireplace and be decorated for the Christmas season with holly and mistletoe. When she entered, every eye would turn to see who it was. They would all gaze at her admiringly, the young men especially, with her lovely green silk gown trimmed with ribbon roses, her dainty satin slippers, and more jewelry than she'd ever worn—a pearl necklace, pearl earrings, and strands of pearls woven into her hair. Then the musicians would pick up their flutes and fiddles and she would dance and dance all the evening, until she could dance no more.

She felt a sudden urge to look at her gown again, to feel the silky fabric against her skin. She poked one foot out from under the covers but just as quickly drew it back again. It was cozy and warm under the covers, but her room was bitterly cold!

Of course it was cold, so early in the morning, with the fire gone cold. Maybe she should just stay in bed until Jane came to light the fire?

Don't be such a ninny, she told herself sternly. Are you afraid of a little cold? She forced herself to throw back the covers and leapt out of bed. For a moment she just stood there, shivering in her thin linen shift. Then she looked at her ball gown, hanging there on a wooden peg on the wall, and made her way across the room.

Amanda slipped on the gown and held it tight against her. Then she danced barefoot in the moonlight around the room, imagining herself at the ball. Round and round she danced, as light and graceful as a swallow, until she was brought back to earth by her mother's voice.

"Amanda! Breakfast is ready, where are you? Are you still sleeping, you lazy thing?"

"I'm coming, Mother, just a moment," she called back to her. Her mother didn't sound really angry, but Amanda hurriedly took off the gown and scurried to get dressed in her normal clothes.

She needed help with her stays, though—where was Jane? She was awfully late coming up to her room. Just as she was struggling to lace up the stays by herself, Jane came in at last. Jane was a new servant, just come over from Ireland. She could have been attractive, with her dark eyes and her long dark hair, if she wasn't always looking mean and scowling. She was scowling now.

"Where have you been? It's awfully late, you know!"

As soon she said it, Amanda was sorry for the sharpness of her tone. Jane was so much older than she was (she must have been well past twenty) that it seemed disrespectful. And maybe Jane just made a mistake, because she hadn't been a servant very long. She'd wanted to come to Virginia from Ireland, so she'd agreed to work to pay her fare. She'd work for six years for someone—whoever bought her agreement from the captain—and they she'd be free and on her own. It was called being an "indentured servant" and a lot of people came over to Virginia that way.

"Well I'm here now, aren't I?" Jane said crossly, roughly turning Amanda around so she could get at the back of the stays where the lacing was. As she laced them up, she pulled the string tighter and tighter and tighter—so tight, that Amanda could hardly breathe.

"Looser, please!" Amanda cried, but Jane only gave an especially vicious tug and pulled it even tighter. So Amanda took a deep breath to make her chest as big as possible, held it while Jane finished off the lacing, and then let it out only when she was done.

Amanda put on her own petticoat and a clean white neck handkerchief around her shoulders, and then Jane helped her into her gown. Now she was nearly dressed.

"Thank you, Jane, I can do the rest myself." Amanda tried to sound as firm and dignified as her mother always did when speaking to servants. "You can light the fire now."

"Whatever you say, *Miss* Amanda." Jane sneered and pretended to curtsey, in the most mocking, sarcastic way.

"That's not very nice you know." Amanda was feeling pretty ill-used, to tell the truth. "Even if you are older than I am. My mother's very particular that everyone should treat each other with respect."

"Your 'mother,' that's what you call her?" Jane had an odd little smile on her face, as if she knew some secret but she wouldn't tell. "How very peculiar."

Then she turned her back on Amanda and knelt down by the fire to light it.

Amanda stared at her, feeling strangely disturbed. What an odd thing to say! Didn't every child call their parents "Mother" and "Father?" Of course, calling them "Mr. and Mrs. Lambertson" was more correct and formal. Maybe that's what she meant?

"Amanda!" Mrs. Lambertson called up the stairs again.

"I'm coming!" Shaking her head to dispel her puzzlement, Amanda left her room and ran down to her.

"How many times must I tell you to walk, Amanda?" Mrs. Lambertson scolded her as she bounded down the bottom stair. She stood just outside the dining room in the hallway, a slim woman in a white and blue gown, with a fine gauze cap covering her chestnut-colored hair. Usually she was happy and smiling, but now she shook her head disapprovingly.

"Amanda, breakfast is ready"

"You're a young lady now, not a child. You must learn to behave like one."

"Yes Mother," Amanda answered obediently, and she took her place at the table.

As she ate her bread and cold leftover ham, Jane's strange and challenging words came back to trouble her.

She almost told her mother about it, but she felt oddly reluctant to do so. Looking at her, sitting there across from her at the table, she had a sudden vision of another woman's face, a sad, pale face surrounded by rust-red hair like her own. It was a dim sort of picture, vague and fuzzy around the edges, like a forgotten bit of dream. And like a dream, it quickly vanished, and once again she saw her mother's familiar features.

chapter 2

The ball was every bit as wonderful as Amanda had imagined. The carriage ride was wonderful, gliding over the snow-crusted ground in the moon-light, and Mr. and Mrs. Hunt's plantation house was bright and warm. It smelled of wood smoke, with sprigs of mistletoe and holly all over, and it was cheerfully full of the many other guests who had already arrived.

Everyone looked so glamorous, all dressed up for the holidays in their fanciest clothes. Men and women, young and old, wore their very best silks, velvets, and satins, sparkling in the candle-light with their sequin trims, their gold and silver laces, their shoe-buckles and earrings and necklaces of gold and silver, diamonds and

Everyone looked so glamorous

pearls. Some of the guests were already in the ballroom
dancing, while others drank punch and nibbled on sweetmeats, or sat at tables playing card games like whist and
loo. The young men were gallant and the young women

coyly flirting, everyone smiling and laughing and having the best of times.

Amanda didn't know anyone very well but it didn't matter. They welcomed her like a long-lost friend. Soon she was part of the whirling dancers, and she danced every dance. She danced most of all with a young boy named Edmund, Mrs. Hunt's visiting cousin. He was dark-haired and good-looking, with sparkling eyes and a ready smile. He was only just twelve — his birthday was only a few days before hers — and was visiting from Richmond. At first he was shy and awkward, but they got along quite famously. Soon they both forgot to be shy, and they were talking and laughing like they'd known each other forever.

About halfway through the ball, the Twelfth Night cakes were served. There was a Queen's Cake for the ladies, full of raisins and apples and covered with white sugar icing flavored with rosewater. Mrs. Hunt told everyone proudly that she'd gotten the recipe from Mrs. Washington herself. The gentlemen had a King's Cake, fragrant with nutmeg, cinnamon, and brandy. It was the tradition for each to contain, hidden somewhere within it, a small bean or a bead or a charm. The lady and gentleman who found them in their slices of cake would be crowned the Queen and King of the ball and dance a minuet together.

"I've done something new this year," Mrs. Hunt announced to the guests as the cake was being served. "I hope you don't mind something different. The ones who get the little crown charms will be the King and Queen, but I've included some other charms as well. The ones who get them will get a fortune for the year to come."

No one seemed to mind at all. To the contrary. Hoping they'd gotten a fortune charm, the guests ate their cake all the more eagerly.

"Oh, I have one!" Amanda called out happily, as her fork encountered something hard. She ate away around it carefully, until the charm was revealed. It was a little ship. She looked around at all the others. Some were smiling and showing their charms around. Others looked at their empty plates, disappointed.

After all the charms were found it was time to crown the King and Queen. The King was Edmund, Mrs. Hunt's cousin, and he looked proud but comical in his gilded paper crown. He bowed gracefully to the Queen — a young girl from Williamsburg Amanda hadn't seen before — and they danced a minuet together. They must both have excellent dancing masters, thought Amanda, as they made it through the complicated dance most elegantly, without a single mistake.

The ceremony, however, was not yet over. As soon as the minuet music ended, Mr. Hunt called the assembly to order.

"Attention everyone!" He waved a sheet of paper in the air. "Now I'll interpret your fortunes. Come over here, everyone who has a charm."

"I have a ring," a young lady in a pink silk gown called out gaily.

Mr. Hunt consulted his piece of paper.

"A ring — that means you'll get married this year!"

She glanced at the young man standing by her side and blushed scarlet, setting everyone off laughing.

A blond young man in a blue silk outfit made his way forward through the crowd.

"I have a sword. Does that mean I'll be a soldier?"

He turned to an attractive young woman standing nearby him.

"Alas, milady, I must say my goodbyes," he spoke with exaggerated emphasis, like an actor in a play, and looked very solemn. "I'm off to foreign lands, leaving my family and home behind me."

He took the young lady's hand in his, lifted it to his lips, and kissed it gallantly.

"I doubt it means that," Mr. Hunt told him, chuckling. "Aren't you turning eighteen this year? Most likely it only means you'll be joining your father's militia."

The young man made a comical face and shrugged, drawing a laugh from the audience.

"This young lady has a charm as well," Edmund called out, gesturing to Amanda. Shyly, she came forward and showed Mr. Hunt her charm.

"What's this? A ship, is it? Hmm." Mr. Hunt looked at his paper. "We must have mixed up the charms — this should have been in the King's cake, not the Queen's cake. It's a charm for a gentleman, not a young lady."

"But what does it mean?" Amanda asked shyly.

"It says there's a sailing ship in your future." He cocked his head and studied her, as if trying to imagine it, and then shook his head. "I'm very much afraid, my dear, that this time the fortunes have failed us. Try as I might, I can't quite picture you as a sailor."

Everyone laughed again, and then the other fortunes were told, one after another. There was a shoe, for learning a trade (this brought a laugh, for the gentleman's father owned half the county), and a rose (for the fairest young lady) — all very much what you'd expect. It seemed that only Amanda's ship was the odd one.

After the fortunes the guests resumed their dancing, eating and drinking, and playing cards. All too soon, as it seemed, the ball was over and Amanda was being helped back into her carriage. The ride back home was even more delightfully enchanted than the ride to the ball had been, if that was possible. Already half asleep, Amanda remembered every moment of the evening. It was all like a wonderful dream — the music, the sweetmeats, the dancing, and Edmund with his dark hair and sparkling eyes.

All good things must end in time, but for Amanda that night the time came all too soon. When she got to her room there was Jane, waiting to help undress her and frowning for all she was worth.

"It's about time!" Jane greeted her rudely.

Amanda said nothing and submitted to her ministrations, hoping that Jane would soon be done and gone, and she could go back to reliving the evening.

"She's at the ball, like a fine little lady, and what about me?" Jane muttered, as she undid the hooks on the gown and the ties on the petticoat. She was pretending to be talking to herself, but she knew full well that Amanda could hear her. "I'm just waiting and waiting. And her just a common girl like me, pretending she's someone special!"

"Whatever do you mean?" Amanda couldn't help but ask, despite her resolution to say nothing. "I'm sorry you had to stay up, but what are you talking about?"

Jane gave Amanda a look, as if she knew more but wasn't going to say it.

"It's not my place to say, so go ask your 'mother,' as you call her." She finished unlacing Amanda's stays and walked toward the door. "Now I can get some sleep myself. Good night to you, *Miss* Amanda."

Amanda lay awake for a long while afterwards, replaying in her mind every moment of the evening. But her thoughts kept coming back to Jane. Whatever did she mean — "a common girl like me, pretending she's someone special"?

chapter 3

The next day, Amanda avoided Jane as much as possible. Every time they were together, Jane always said something nasty or strange. How she wished Jane hadn't come to her home, that she'd never even come to Virginia!

Amanda's mother seemed to think that Jane should be her lady's maid, and help her dress and everything. Amanda tried to tell her mother that she didn't want Jane to be the one helping her, but her mother didn't understand.

"Can someone else help me, besides Jane?" she asked over breakfast.

The question clearly surprised Mrs. Lambertson.

"Why not? Is something wrong?"

It was a reasonable question, but what to answer? What had Jane said to her, really? So much was in the way she said it. The words didn't seem to mean so much, standing alone. Wouldn't her mother think she was imagining things, or exaggerating?

"She isn't nice to me," Amanda said finally. "She's rude and she's mean."

Mrs. Lambertson didn't think that was a very good reason.

"She's not used to being a servant, that's all. You must be patient and teach her. She hasn't been a servant very long."

"But she —"

"Your mother's right," Mr. Lambertson broke in. "You mustn't be so particular. I'm sure she'll learn before too long."

And that was the end of the conversation.

Amanda managed to avoid Jane for one whole day, and most of the day after. Then they had a real confrontation, on account of Emily.

Emily's mother was the cook, and Emily did whatever chores she could around the kitchen, like bringing in sticks of firewood, washing up, and sweeping. She was barely six years old, but she was the only other child in the household. She was the only companion Amanda had, and she cared for Emily like a younger sister. Whenever she could she'd play with the child — when Amanda had a moment free and Emily did too. Amanda gave Emily one of her own dolls and made little clothes for it, and she made up silly little games to play and funny stories to tell her.

Emily would be leaving the Lambertsons in a month, and Amanda hated to think of it. The cook was leaving for another job, far away in Charlottesville.

That day, Emily was sweeping out the fireplace. That was one of her jobs, to gather up the ashes from the fire. They were used to make soap and to fertilize the plants in the garden. Emily had a tiny broom and she was sweeping

a bit too enthusiastically. She swept up a cloud of ashes just as Jane was walking by. Some of them — a tiny few it was, really — got onto Jane's apron and dirtied it.

"Stupid little girl," Jane yelled. She slapped Emily hard on the cheek, and then grabbed onto her little arms and shook her. "Just see what you've done to me!" She gave the child an angry shove, and poor Emily fell onto the stone hearth in front of the fireplace.

Amanda was passing by the kitchen house when it happened. She happened to look inside and see, and she immediately ran up to them.

"Stop it!" she cried. "She's just a little girl — what have you done to her?" She hadn't meant to speak to Jane ever again if she could help it, but she was so upset the words just came out. Jane gave her an evil look and stalked away.

Amanda didn't say anything more, but Emily told her mother. And her mother told the housekeeper, and Jane got in trouble.

The next time Jane saw Amanda, her eyes flashed like she meant to murder her. "You'll be sorry," Jane whispered menacingly, and Amanda knew she was in for it.

It started that very evening.

Usually Mrs. Lambertson would brush Amanda's hair and say goodnight, but tonight she was too busy. So Jane came up instead, with a sly, secret smile that gave

Amanda the shivers. Jane didn't say a word at first, but as she brushed Amanda's hair, the strokes came more and more fiercely. The bristles were stiff, and as Jane dug them into Amanda's scalp, it was starting to hurt her.

Amanda bore it for a while without saying a word. She didn't want another fight — not tonight, not ever. She just wanted Jane to finish brushing her hair and leave her. But Jane only brushed harder and harder, as if she was deliberately trying to cause her pain. Soon she was slamming the brush down so hard that Amanda was getting a headache. If this went on much longer, she thought, her scalp would start bleeding!

"Stop! You're hurting me!" Amanda cried out finally. "You're trying to hurt me, I know you are! I didn't tell on you about Emily, but it was a mean and awful thing to do and I'm glad you got in trouble! You're a horrible person, you are — ever since you came here, you've been just horrible!"

"So I'm horrible, am I?" Jane snapped back, brushing harder still. "So something's wrong with me? You're a fine one to talk! You ought to be grateful I'm brushing it at all. Do you think you deserve all this?" She gestured widely at Amanda's large room, her nice warm bed, her ball gown. "Well I'll tell you, you don't deserve a bit of it! You don't deserve your fancy room and your fancy clothes, no more than I do. You're just a servant girl, like me! Mr. Lambertson isn't your father, you know — and Mrs. Lambertson isn't your mother!"

Amanda was so stunned, she couldn't say a word. Jane saw it and smiled in satisfaction.

"That's right, you're just a silly little fool," she said, "and I'm glad to be the one to tell you. Someday your luck will change, and the magistrate will take it all away from you. You'll be a servant again, just like me. I can hardly wait to see it!"

Jane dropped the brush on the floor and stalked out of the room, leaving Amanda sitting there in her shift, shocked and frightened.

Amanda crept slowly into her bed but she couldn't think of sleeping. She just lay there, her thoughts in a dreadful turmoil. What did Jane mean? Was she making things up, trying to upset her? If that was what she was trying to do, she'd certainly succeeded! But what if it all was true — could it possibly be true? About the Lambertsons not being her parents, about her being a servant?

The next day she crept about the house in a daze, pale and frightened. She'd decided that somehow Jane must be right. She'd sounded so sure of herself, so certain! But what did it all mean? If Mrs. Lambertson wasn't her mother, who was, and where was she? Would the magistrate really take her away from home, as Jane had threatened? Or could Mr. and Mrs. Lambertson send her away, if they were unhappy with her? Suddenly she felt so lonely and afraid — if she had to leave the Lambertsons, what would become of her?

It was late afternoon when John the Gardener found her crying in the garden. He was pruning shrubs, but he came right over to her when he heard her sobbing. She turned her face away when she saw him coming, but it didn't fool him.

He was pruning shrubs

"Now Miss Amanda, why are you crying? You can tell old John," he said kindly.

Amanda was afraid to tell him, but he already knew. Jane had been bragging to the other servants, saying how she'd told Amanda "a thing or two" and she was proud of it. She'd recounted their entire conversation, nearly word-for-word.

"It's what Jane said isn't it?" he said gently.

Amanda sniffled and nodded.

"You shouldn't pay her any mind," he said firmly.

"But why is she always so mean to me? Did I do something to her, that I don't know about?"

"It's nothing you've done," John reassured her. "She's like that with everybody. She's only jealous, that's all it is. Some people can't help but blame others for what they don't have, is what it seems like."

"But is it true what she says?" Amanda hardly dared to ask, but she couldn't go on just wondering and worrying. "About the magistrate and everything? She said the magistrate would take everything away. And she seemed to say Mrs. Lambertson wasn't even my mother!"

John looked at her, amazed.

"Mrs. Lambertson never told you? You really don't know? "

Amanda shook her head.

He stared at her. He certainly didn't want to be the one to tell her! But she was in such a state, he could hardly bear it. And he knew that if he didn't do something, Jane would go on tormenting her.

"Jane's right that Mrs. Lambertson's not your mother. Your real mother died long ago." He said it as gently as he could. Then he stopped and waited to see how she would take it.

It was as if she'd been turned to stone. She sat there as still as a statute, staring off into space and hardly breathing. It was like the ground had opened up beneath her feet, and she'd fallen in a deep, dark hole. Her worst fears had been realized.

At last she drew a deep breath and looked at John.

"Go on," she said bravely. "You must tell it all."

John swore he'd make Jane pay for ever starting this. He could see he had no choice but to continue.

"Your real mother died, as I said, when you was very young. You wasn't but about this high, when you came here —" he held his hand about two feet off the ground, "and as sweet as honey."

Amanda felt a deep stabbing pain of grief and sadness. Her real mother was dead! Was hers the sad, pale face she sometimes remembered, the woman with hair like her own? "But what about my father? Why didn't I stay with him?"

"Your father was a sailor, my girl," he said simply, as if that explained it. And it did. A sailor was never home, he had to be always off sailing. "He didn't know no other life, so he had to leave you."

Amanda just stared at him, amazed. Another mother, and another father too? She remembered the ship, the Queen's Cake charm—was that what it meant, that her father was a sailor?

"Where is my father now?" she asked finally.

The gardener shook his head.

"There's no telling. Some faraway place most likely, maybe India or even China. Those ships go everywhere. He could even be lost at sea, washed overboard."

"Lost at sea?!"

"Most likely not," he said quickly, seeing how he'd upset her. "But wherever he is, he couldn't take you with him. There's no young girls at sea." He looked at her, to see if she was following. She nodded briefly, to show that she understood him.

"So, anyway," he went on reluctantly, "when there's an orphan, or a child whose parents can't take care of it, the court sends them out to someone else, to teach them a trade and raise them."

Amanda was beginning to take it all in, and it frightened her.

"You mean Jane's right? I came here as a servant?"

"It's not quite the same," John said thoughtfully. "I don't know much about the law, but I think it's more like being an apprentice. But don't worry yourself there, that's only what they call a technicality. It didn't turn out that way, on account of Mrs. Lambertson."

"Mrs. Lambertson?"

"She'd always wanted a daughter so much, but she never had any children. And you being so pretty and sweet, she immediately took you to her heart. You were a daughter she'd always prayed for. 'Heaven's gift to me,' she said — I heard her with my own ears." He gave Amanda a knowing look and a friendly nudge. "Wouldn'a been that way if you was Jane, that's for sure. She's been mean and sour I reckon, since the day she was born, and she never had a sweet word for anyone."

Amanda felt as if an evil spell had bewitched her. But no, she realized — it was in the past that she'd been bewitched, under a spell of ignorance. This news, this terrible news — this was the reality.

"But what about the magistrate taking it all away?" she managed to whisper.

"Never in your life!" John said firmly. "You're a daughter to Mrs. Lambertson now, and I'm sure she couldn't bear to part with you. You'll stay until some fine young man comes along to marry you. And don't you worry about Jane," he added grimly. "I'll see that she don't trouble you no more, I promise you."

They were reassuring words, but could she believe them?

chapter 4

Amanda never knew what John said to Jane. Whatever he said, it worked for a little while. After that talk in the garden, and for a few days after. For a change, it was Jane who avoided Amanda, and not the other way around. When they did happen to run into each other, Jane bowed her head and scurried on by.

Between Amanda and the Lambertsons, everything remained the same on the surface. Amanda still called Mrs. Lambertson "Mother" and Mr. Lambertson "Father," like she always had, and she didn't say a word about what John had told her. She still thought of them as her mother and father too, only now she had another father too — to herself, she called him "sailor father." Sometimes she forgot that anything had changed, and things seemed the same as ever. More often, though, she felt as if she'd been dreaming all her life and she'd only just awoken.

Late at night, lying in her bed, she'd allow herself to think of all the questions that she refused to think about during daylight. She had another mother, a different mother than she'd ever known — was that the face she'd seen, that she thought she'd only just imagined?

And a different father too! What did he look like? Was he fair like her? Was he short and ugly, or tall and handsome? Was he even still alive? He must be!

She imagined him standing on the deck of a tall-masted ship, and herself standing there beside him. Together they'd sail and sail over the endless ocean, to China and beyond, in search of exotic goods — silks and porcelain and tea, cinnamon and nutmeg and other costly spices.

Unfortunately for Amanda, Jane quickly recovered her bad attitude. It wasn't even a week before she showed up in Amanda's room first thing in the morning, as mean as ever.

"Mrs. Lambertson says I'm to help you get dressed and then fix your hair. *Miss* Amanda," she greeted Amanda in her mocking way. "I'm sure you'll enjoy it."

Amanda didn't say anything at all. She bore it, rough handling, tight stays and all, and got dressed in silence.

"So John told you I was right, didn't he?" Jane said triumphantly as she fussed with Amanda's hair, pulling it hard as she arranged the curls this way and that way.

"You weren't right at all," Amanda answered her firmly. "Not about anything that mattered. He said it wasn't like you — I'm an apprentice, not a servant, and even that's not it — it's only what they call a technicality. The magistrate would never take me away, because I really am just like a daughter to the Lambertsons."

"Shows what he knows!" Jane snorted her contempt for the gardener. "And as for its being an apprenticeship, that's even worse! There's rules and conditions for apprentices, about how you're supposed to treat them, and the Lambertson's aren't doing what they're supposed to. You're supposed to be working at a trade, for one thing. Learning a way to make a living, for one thing. And what trade are you learning? It's a joke, not a trade, pretending you're a fine lady."

"I know all kinds of things!" Amanda said hotly. She turned to face Jane head on, emboldened by her anger. "I know a lot more than you do! I can read and write and do sums — can you? I can speak foreign languages! I can play music, and dance, and write poetry!"

Jane snorted again, even more loudly.

"Poetry? You'll have a fine time earning your living with poetry! That's what you'll have to do, you know. That's how it is with apprentices. Once you're grown you'll have to go away from here. You'll be on your own then, forever more, and who will pay you to write poetry?"

"I don't believe a word you say!" Amanda said stoutly. "You're just trying to upset me. I may not be their real daughter, but they love me just the same. And I can fix my own hair from now on, thank you!"

Amanda took the pins right out of Jane's hand and threw them down hard on the dressing table. Some of them slid over the edge and fell on the floor, but she didn't even look at them.

"You're just jealous, that's what you are!" Amanda was nearly in tears, she was so angry. "Jealous and mean and spiteful!"

Watching Jane as she left the room, all self-righteous and huffy, Amanda felt a thrill of relief and triumph for standing up to her. At the same time, however, her heart felt numb with worry.

Jane had been right about everything before. Could she be right again, even partly? If she wasn't really the Lambertson's daughter, they didn't have to keep her, did they? Wasn't her fate really in the hands of the court? However fine things seemed right now, could everything change in a moment?

chapter 5

Nothing more happened the next day, and the next day after. Amanda had almost convinced herself that she was being foolish to worry so, when she heard something that confirmed the very worst she had imagined.

She was passing by Mr. Lambertson's study, on the way to go outside, when she heard angry voices arguing. One voice was Mr. Lambertson's, but she was pretty sure she'd never heard the other man's voice before. They were talking so loudly that even though the door was closed, she could hear what they were saying.

Amanda didn't usually eavesdrop on Mr. Lambertson's affairs, but after everything Jane had said, she couldn't help but be nervous and uneasy. She had to know what the argument was about, so she stood there in the hallway, listening.

"I won't give her up," Mr. Lambertson was saying grimly. "After all that's gone on, all this time, you should know that I'll fight to keep her!"

"Well then, I'll see you in court, if you won't part with her otherwise!" shouted the voice of the stranger. "Then we'll see what the magistrate has to say. I'm the one with the law on my side. You'll be sorry!"

The door slammed open and the man burst out into the hallway. Amanda didn't have time to hide, but it didn't matter. He stalked angrily to the front door and stormed out, never looking behind him.

Mr. Lambertson followed behind and watched his departure, shaking his head sadly. Then he noticed Amanda standing there and gave a start.

"Amanda! What are you doing?"

Amanda stared guiltily at the floor.

"I didn't mean to listen in. I was just passing by on my way outside. "

Mr. Lambertson looked at her sadly. He seemed awfully, terribly worried.

"Put it out of your mind," he said evenly. "It's nothing. Let him go to court; he'll never win. The man's a fool and a hothead." He turned and went back into his study, shutting the door firmly behind him.

Amanda stood there for a moment puzzling over it all, when she heard a loud laugh from somewhere down the hallway behind her. Jane had been eavesdropping too and she had a nasty look of triumph.

Jane had been eavesdropping too

"There you see, what did I say! I'm right again! That's Mr. Pryor the brickmaker, and he's going to court to get you! He'll tell them the Lambertsons aren't teaching you a trade like they're supposed to. He wants you to come make bricks I expect — there's a trade for you. I hear he needs help to make bricks for the wall around the churchyard. It's the church, you know, that's responsible for orphans. It's the church that has the final say on where you are and what you do, and it's the church that needs the bricks so badly. So the court will surely take you away and give you to Mr. Pryor!"

Jane moved closer to Amanda and dropped her voice to an evil whisper.

"Brick making's terrible hard work, I hear, hard and dirty. But it's all you're good for, with your music and French and poetry. Your pretty little hands will be rough and red from mixing the clay, and your body will be crippled and aching from all that endless bending and lifting. You'll envy me my servant's job then! I can't wait to see it."

"You're just making it up," Amanda said haughtily, backing away from her. "You're a mean, stupid girl who can't even read and write, and you don't know anything."

Jane just turned her back and went off down the hall, laughing.

Amanda pretended she didn't care, but inside Jane's words ate away at her. Mr. Pryor said he was going to court and he sounded like he meant it. From what she'd heard, once someone went to court, you could never be sure what would happen. She'd heard Mr. Lambertson himself complained about it. And what Jane said about the church was true—how the church cared for orphans and how they needed people to make bricks for the churchyard. So it all made sense, that the magistrate would agree, and give her to Mr. Pryor.

It was a horrible thought, almost too horrible to contemplate! It wasn't just the hard work making bricks—that she could have lived with. But leaving Mr. and Mrs. Lambertson, and the only home she'd ever known, that would break her heart. And to belong to that man, to have him in charge of her! Mr. Lambertson called him a hothead and a fool, and he was cruel and violent too, from the looks of him!

In the days that followed, Amanda looked anxiously for any sign, any hint, that Mr. Pryor would do what he threatened. Whenever there was a messenger bringing a paper, or any other delivery from the outside world, she tried to find out its contents. Whenever Mr. Lambertson had a visitor in his study, she found an excuse to linger nearby and try to overhear what they were saying.

Her worst fears were confirmed a few days later, when Mr. Lambertson's legal partner Mr. Wilkerson came to call. She was too late to hear the beginning of the conversation but the part she did hear was more than enough.

"I heard that Mr. Pryor has gone to court," Mr. Wilkerson was saying.

"That's right," Mr. Lambertson said grimly. "The man's a monster."

"He may win, you know," Mr. Wilkerson warned him. "You may have the right on your side, but I'm afraid he's got the law on his side."

"I can't believe they'd take her away," Mr. Lambertson said heatedly, "it would be cruel and outrageous!"

Mr. Lambertson's voice grew even louder.

"Well, I just hope you're right," Wilkerson replied, "but I'm afraid the magistrate will agree with him."

Amanda was holding her breath, so as not to miss a word of what they were saying. After that, however, the conversation turned to other matters.

She stood there for a long time in the hallway, terrified and miserable. Finally she roused herself, went up to her room, and curled up on her bed. She felt too terrible even to cry. She stayed there until supper and then she went downstairs. She was pale and wan, looking like she might faint dead away at any moment.

"What on earth is the matter with you?" Mrs. Lambertson asked her, as soon as she saw her.

"Oh, Mother, I love you so!" was all that Amanda could answer. And she went over to Mrs. Lambertson and hugged her so hard she could hardly breathe.

"Well, I do say!" Mrs. Lambertson stroked Amanda's hair, deeply touched but also mystified by her behavior. "I love you too, my dear girl. Now come, let's eat supper."

Two days later Mr. Lambertson went off to Williamsburg. Amanda had gathered from little things she overheard that it was the day of decision for the lawsuit.

When Mr. Lambertson left, he was in the best of spirits, looking jaunty and sure of success. When he returned, however, he looked depressed and dejected. He went straight to his office and called for Mrs. Lambertson to come, and they spoke softly together.

Amanda tried to listen but she couldn't make out what they were saying. And then, nearly as soon as they'd gone into the office and shut the door, there was Jane, poking her head around the corner. Of course it was no accident that Jane happened to be there just then. She must have been looking out, just like Amanda, waiting for Mr. Lambertson to come home again.

When he returned, he looked depressed

"Ha!" she smirked, "I was right, wasn't I? That's the end of you, my fine little lady." She turned and went back up the stairs, humming a little tune and laughing.

Amanda felt a growing resolve as she stood there in the hallway after Jane's departure. This time, Jane wouldn't be right! This time, she wouldn't just be passive when faced with disaster! She would run away that very night. She wouldn't, she couldn't ever be that awful man's apprentice.

chapter 6

It wasn't a very practical idea to run away, but then Amanda wasn't thinking very clearly. All she knew was, she couldn't just sit there and wait until the sheriff came and dragged her off. She had a vague idea that if she could only hide out for a while, some days or even a week or two, everything would turn out all right. She didn't know how exactly, but maybe Mr. Lambertson would somehow be able to change the magistrate's decision. Or if not, maybe she could make her way to another town and find herself a place as a servant. Whatever she did — even hiding in the woods, however, hungry, cold and miserable — would be better than the future she faced now, being sent away to Mr. Pryor!

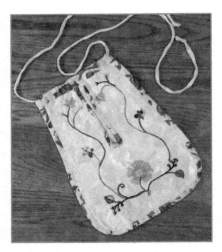

In her pocket

She went to bed as usual, but then lay there until everyone was asleep. It wasn't hard to stay awake. She was so anxious and terrified that she couldn't have slept a wink anyway. When the household was finally all in bed and the house was still and quiet, she rose and noiselessly began to dress herself. She cast a last, lingering look at her ball gown, still hanging on its peg, but she knew she had to leave it behind her. She needed her warmest and most practical clothes to run away, not a fancy silk ball gown.

She put on her linsey-woolsey under-petticoat, and then a quilted wool one, and over them both an old linen petticoat that was patched and worn — the one she wore when she helped John in the garden. She put on her sturdiest shoes and her heavy wool stockings, her oldest wool gown, and a bedgown over it. Her knitted mitts and her red wool cape completed her outfit.

She stuffed two extra pairs of stockings and a pair of riding gloves in her pocket. And the little Queen's Cake ship charm — perhaps that would bring some luck to her.

That went in her pocket too, along with 10 shillings and five pence that she'd gotten as a present for her birthday. She took a large handkerchief as well, to wrap up some bread, cold meat, and dried apples from the kitchen.

It was a moonlit night with a crust of snow on the ground, much like the night of the ball. It was all (or so it seemed) so very long ago. That night, riding along in the carriage in the moonlight, the forest had seemed silvery-bright and magical. Tonight, however, alone and on foot, it was full of twisted shapes and dangerous-looking shadows, looming up to grab at her in the dark. She didn't have any second thoughts though about her resolution. Anything was better than what lay in store for her at home.

It was late and she didn't expect to get very far, not in the cold and the darkness. She remembered, however, how once she'd passed a small abandoned shed when she was riding with her mother to visit the nearest neighbors. She thought it wasn't so very far, but she hadn't really been paying close attention. As it turned out, it was a lot farther than she remembered.

It took her over an hour of painful progress, stumbling over roots and pushing her way through brambles, before she finally saw it. It was a rickety wooden shed overgrown with vines and falling apart with disrepair, but it was shelter. The relief was so great that it brought tears to her eyes. As tired as she was, she went right in and curled up on the floor, ignoring the dirt, the holes in the walls, and the rotting, broken floorboards. It wasn't the kind of bed she was used to, and she was pretty sure that at least one small creature was sleeping there also. Still, it was better than sleeping on the bare ground, out in the open. She wrapped her cloak tightly around her and went to sleep.

It was a rickety wooden shed

Maybe it was because the many days of anxiety and emotion had drained her energy, or maybe just because she'd gone to sleep so late, but she slept long and soundly. When she woke at last the next morning, the sun was high in the sky. She was cold, stiff, and hungry.

She ate some of the bread and meat she'd brought along and then looked glumly at what was left over. It wasn't much. She'd already eaten half the food she brought with her for breakfast. If only she'd thought to bring much more! With a sigh, she wrapped up what was left in her handkerchief and put it back in her pocket. She tried to remember what she'd learned from the gardener John about wild food in the forest. Several times he'd taken her into the forest to teach her the names of the plants and trees. Was there anything she could eat, any leaves or roots or berries that were safe to eat, that she could find this time of year? She wished she'd paid more attention to what he'd told her! Maybe if she went exploring, she could find something that looked familiar and remember what he said?

Exploring at least got her moving and that warmed her. The sun was shining and the patches of snow were melting, here and there. All in all, she passed the day rather pleasantly, but she didn't find anything that she dared eat for her supper. Come tomorrow, she had to move on. She was hungry, her food was gone, and she had to find some better hiding place.

The second night in the little shed, her sleep was fitful and uneasy. One time, a sort of scrabbling noise awakened her and she saw two yellow eyes in the doorway, looking back at her in the dark. She finally got back to sleep, only to have a nightmare. She dreamt she was imprisoned in a sailing ship, weighted down with in heavy chains in the very bottom of the hold. She could hear the sounds of a life-and-death struggle above her — the gunfire, the clash of swords, and the shouts of angry men. She heard the loud boom of a cannon, and then a cannonball hit the side of the ship. It burst through the planking just beside her.

The water started rushing in, and Jane was standing there beside her. Jane had the key to unlock her chains, but of course she didn't do it. "I can swim," she cried, laughing as the water rose higher, "but you will drown!"

So Amanda could do nothing but sit there, held fast by her heavy chains, as the water was rising higher and higher around her. She woke up just before it covered her face. Thank heaven! She opened her eyes, and saw Gardner John standing at the open doorway.

chapter 7

Amanda's flight had been discovered almost immediately the next morning. Jane had gone up light the fire and saw that Amanda's bed and bedroom were empty. Maybe she'd felt guilty, or maybe she was only afraid of being blamed for it, but either way she'd run right back downstairs and told the Lambertsons Amanda was missing.

Needless to say, all the men in the household started searching immediately. Amanda's mother desperately wanted to join them, but her husband insisted she must stay home.

"One of us has to be here," he told her. "What if someone comes with news of her? What if she comes home?"

Mrs. Lambertson couldn't help but agree. She knew what he said was sensible. So she waited all alone in the parlor.

The searching was all in vain, though they searched all day long and well into the evening. Only when it was too dark to see did they finally come home. They hadn't found any trace of her.

All night long, Mr. and Mrs. Lambertson were mad with worry — she was a young girl, out there in the cold and dark all alone, maybe lost, or maybe injured or dying.

The next morning they set forth again, even before sunrise. This time, John the Gardner thought to go looking on his own. He'd remembered their walks in the woods together and a memory of the old abandoned shed came back to him.

When he brought her home, Mr. and Mrs. Lambertson held her long and closely. Then the questions began.

"Why, Amanda, why did you do it?" Mrs. Lambertson asked in anguish.

"Are you so unhappy here?" Mr. Lambertson asked sadly.

"I didn't want them to take me!" Amanda clung to them, sobbing. "Please don't let them take me away!"

"What on earth are you talking about?" Mr. Lambertson looked at her in amazement.

Then it all came out in a rush, and not very clearly.

She waited all alone

"It was on account of the lawsuit!" Amanda looked at Mrs. Lambertson through her tears, her eyes wide and pleading. "Why didn't you tell me — I never knew — that I wasn't really your daughter? Now the magistrate will take me away, and give me to Mr. Pryor!"

"Oh my dear, I'm so sorry! I should have told you!" Mrs. Lambertson looked stricken. "I meant to, I really did. I kept telling myself that I would, but I couldn't do it. I was afraid it would change things."

"But why did you think anyone would take you away?" Mr. Lambertson broke in, sorely puzzled. "What's all this about the magistrate and the lawsuit?"

Forgetting the joy of coming home, Amanda suddenly remembered the grim fate that awaited her.

"Won't the magistrate give me away to Mr. Pryor now, now that he's won his lawsuit?" Mr. Lambertson stared at her in astonishment.

"Mr. Pryor? His lawsuit had nothing to do with you! Whatever put such an idea in your head?"

"You mean it isn't true?" Amanda was so relieved she could hardly believe it. "But you were arguing about a girl — he wanted her, and you were afraid he'd take her, who else could it be? That girl, I mean — wasn't that me you were talking about? Who else could it be?

Mr. Lambertson cradled Amanda's head in his hands and looked at her gravely.

"My dear child, it wasn't you we were talking about at all. We were talking about Penney, one of Mr. Pryor's slaves. She ran away after he — well, I won't go into what he did to her, but even slaves should have some protection, if their master treats them badly enough."

"But you lost, and she had to go back to him?"

Amanda was thrilled to realize she'd been mistaken, but at the same time she felt sorry for poor Penney. She remembered her quite well. She'd been helping out in the kitchen and they'd played games with Emily together. Penney would always let Emily win, and she made them all laugh, telling them funny stories.

"He lied," Mr. Lambertson answered bluntly. "He denied everything. I think the magistrate was suspicious, but it wasn't enough. It's not over though," he added reassuringly. "If he keeps mistreating her, I'll do over and over again until the magistrate agrees with me. He's a decent man, really. He's bound to agree with me, in the end."

"But now that you know the whole story, my dear," he continued, "I hope you feel better? As far as we're concerned, you're our daughter and you always will be. No one will ever take you away from us, I promise you. Not unless you want to."

From the way that he looked at her, and Mrs. Lambertson also, she could see they were afraid that things would change now she knew she wasn't really their daughter.

"Oh no, I never want to leave you!" she cried, embracing them, "that's why I ran away! I thought somehow, if I hid for a while, you'd make everything right again. You're my mother and father, and I love you with all my heart."

She meant every word, but still a voice whispered inside her — "your sailor father, where is he right now? Is he even still alive? Will you ever see him again?"

chapter 8

When Amanda woke the next morning, she knew she had to keep looking for her sailor father. She hadn't the least idea how to go about it. One thing she knew for sure — she didn't want to ask Mr. Lambertson. It would certainly make him very unhappy and Mrs. Lambertson too. She decided to start by asking John the Gardener.

"How does it work? What happens, when a child's an orphan, or their parents can't take care of them?"

John closed his eyes and scratched his ear to aid his concentration. She waited patiently until he spoke again.

"I don't really know all the details, but the Churchwardens must have something to do with it. They're responsible for the poor in the parish, don't you know. And then the court. The court must be the one what does it in the end. I don't think the Churchwardens have that kind of power."

"So what if I wanted to find out about it? Would I ask at the Vestry?"

He had to think really hard about that one. He knew everything about flowers, herbs, vegetables, and fruit trees, how to plant and when to pick and what to do about insects and diseases. This business of binding out children, however, was pretty far outside of what he knew.

"I reckon I'd start with the court myself," he said at last. "The courts must have to keep a record of everything, don't they? In case there's some argument about it, later on."

Williamsburg. That's where she had to go, she realized. Her father had mentioned there was a clerk of the court there. Mr. Waller, his name was, Benjamin Waller. She'd never met the clerk but she'd heard Mr. Lambertson talking about him. He was a good man and he'd been the county clerk for ages and ages. Someday he'd be a magistrate himself, Mr. Lambertson said.

Maybe if she talked to him, he could help her? But how to get there, to talk to him? If running away had taught her anything, it was that she couldn't get anywhere on her own.

Her father was constantly back and forth to Williamsburg, however, being a lawyer himself. Surely he would take her, if she had a good reason to go? It couldn't be just any trip, though. She didn't want him to know of her errand. If he was going to the courthouse himself, it wouldn't do at all.

Every morning, if he was going to Williamsburg (which he did most days), she'd ask him what his business was. He was surprised and pleased by her questions; she'd never taken much interest in his work before. She felt bad about deceiving him, but she kept on. Finally one morning it seemed the time was right.

"I'm off to Williamsburg again," he informed them at breakfast.

"Are you in court then, Father?" she asked anxiously.

"Oh no, the court's not in session now," he informed her kindly. "They only meet a few days a month. My partner Mr. Wilkerson wants to talk about one of our cases, that's all."

"Will you take me with you? I want to go to the milliner's shop. I'm thinking I might like a new hat, and I have some money given to me for my birthday."

He agreed quite readily. Right after breakfast they set forth, and after a pleasant ride they arrived at Williamsburg.

There were so many lovely things

Amanda made it clear she had plenty to do at the milliner's — there were so many different hat styles and trims to consider, to say nothing of all the other lovely things — the fine linen caps with delicate embroidery, the shelves full of fine imported fabrics, tiny enameled boxes in jewel-like colors, and wooden dolls dressed in the latest fashions from France. There were leather gloves, warm winter muffs, and all sorts of earrings and necklaces, as well as dainty lace handkerchiefs, cunning little work bags for one's sewing tools, and jeweled hairpins to decorate one's hair for the ball. She could stay there for hours and hours she told him, just looking at things, so he chuckled and let her go off on her own.

"I'll meet you there at one o'clock," he said, "and we'll go to the Raleigh Tavern. I'll even buy you some apple pudding, if they have it.

She felt a bit guilty again, hiding her true intentions. He was being so kind and trusting. Dining together, just the two of them, was a special treat, and apple pudding was her very favorite.

She wasn't lying, though, she told herself. She did go to the Milliner's and it did take a while. A straw hat of course, and not very large — but what color silk to cover it with? And ribbon trim, to be sure — Mrs. Hunter the milliner assured her it was quite the fashion. But there were so many different ribbons to choose from! Satin and silk, woven in elaborate patterns or covered with embroidery, solids and stripes in every conceivable width and color. To say nothing of the feathers and flowers!

She could have spent hours and hours there, just as she'd told her father, looking everything over and choosing. But the hour grew late and this was her only opportunity, so she hurried down Duke of Gloucester Street to the Courthouse.

As her father had said, the court wasn't in session, but the door was open. She cautiously crept inside and then looked around her. There were four doors leading off from the courtroom but only one of them was open. She walked up to the door very softly and peeked in.

This must be the clerk's office, she quickly decided. The room was small and plain, but very bright. The sunlight was streaming in from two tall arched windows, illuminating a good-sized desk right in front of her and another, smaller table covered in green felt to the side, covered with stacks of books and little piles of papers.

A tall book-case cabinet standing against the wall was filled to overflowing with leather-bound books and stacks of papers. A gigantic leather trunk, full of yet more papers neatly tied with red tape into little bundles lay on the floor beside the desk. Apart from that, there was hardly anything at all in the office — no pictures on the plain white wall nor rug nor floorcloth on the plain wooden floor, only a wooden bench and a couple of straight-backed chairs.

An older man who looked very official was sitting at the desk in front of her. He wore a blue velvet suit of matching jacket and waistcoat and britches and his hair was so carefully curled and powdered that it must have been a wig. He was writing with a quill in a very large journal that lay open before him. He seemed to be concentrating

A gigantic leather trunk lay on the floor

very hard, but he laid down the quill and looked up at her, as soon as she looked at the door.

"Are you Mr. Waller?"

The man pushed his reading spectacles up on his fore-head and looked at her with curiosity.

"I am. And what might your business be?"

"Please, Sir," she answered politely. "I'm told you have records of apprenticed children, is that right?"

"And what would you be wanting with records of apprentices?" he asked. He inspected her closely, his gaze noting particularly how the green, pink, and white striped ribbons exactly matched the colors of her striped silk gown. "A young lady like you?"

Amanda felt a sudden rush of fear as Jane's threatening words came back to her. If she told him she was supposed to be an apprentice instead of the fine lady he thought she was, whatever would he do? Would she be getting the Lambertsons in trouble for not treating her as their daughter and not teaching her a trade? Worse yet, would he think she'd stolen the clothes and run away from her master? Would he call the sheriff to take her off to the gaol, where they kept the prisoners?

She longed to leave, to run away from the courthouse as if she'd never been there, but she knew that if she ran away she'd never know who her original father and mother were. She'd never know her own true history.

"Please, Sir," she said timidly, "It's my own records I'm looking for. I was bound out, they tell me, because my mother died and my father was off at sea."

Mr. Waller's eyebrows rose so high, they disappeared into his powdered wig.

"I see. And what is your name then?"

"Amanda, Sir. Amanda Lambertson. Leastwise, that's the only name I know."

"Mr. Lambertson, the lawyer?"

Amanda drew a quick, startled breath. Why hadn't she foreseen this? Of course the clerk knew him! Mr. Lambertson was regularly in court.

"Please don't tell him I'm asking! It might upset him so!" Amanda pleaded, her words tumbling out in a rush. "You see, I only just learned that I had another father, and Mr. Lambertson's always been like a father to me! And I love him so dearly, I really do."

"I see." Mr. Waller leaned back in his chair and studied her, as if trying to decide what to do. "Those are very old records you're talking about," he said finally. "I don't keep records as old as that here in my office — there'd be papers everywhere and nowhere to sit or stand. We keep them down in the basement, in barrels. It would be quite a job to find them and dig them out."

"Oh," she said sadly, and then she stood for a moment in silence. She felt a great heaviness in her heart. This had been her one chance, the only hope she'd had of finding out about her sailor father.

"But I remember you now," he went on, and her heart leapt up with hope again. "You and your sister."

"My sister?!" Amanda cried out in astonishment.

He nodded.

"Yes, your sister. Amelia, I think her name was. Yes, that was it — Amanda and Amelia Watkins, the two of you. You so young and her even younger. There you were, in your best little gowns, holding onto each other like your lives depended on it, and your father standing there watching you. He looked like his heart would break in two, but there was nothing he could do about it. He said he had to join his ship and sail away the very next morning."

"But where —? But why —?"

"Where are they now?" His eyes were full of sympathy, but he shook his head regretfully. "I'm afraid I can't tell you. He sailed away, and your sister was bound out like you were. It was a shopkeeper and his wife, as I recall, but they moved to Fredericksburg soon after. What happened after that, I couldn't tell you."

Amanda felt faint and her head was buzzing, but somehow she managed to thank him politely and make her way out of the courthouse. She walked slowly back to the milliner's, in such a daze that she hardly knew where she was going. A sister! The thought entranced her. How lovely it was to have a sister of her very own!

She'd just reached the milliner's when Mr. Lambertson arrived, only steps behind her.

"Have you picked out a hat, my dear? Are you ready to go to the tavern?"

With an enormous effort, Amanda turned her mind away from her sister and back to the question of hats.

"I had narrowed it down to two, but I couldn't decide between them," she said shyly. She turned to a young woman, the milliner's assistant, who was standing behind the counter. "Can you show him?"

The woman reached under the counter and brought out two sample hats. One was covered in black silk, with grey and white striped ribbons. The other was covered in white satin and embroidered all over with bright-colored vines and flowers.

"These were the two, I think?" she said, holding them out to her.

Amanda nodded.

The assistant handed them over so Amanda could model them for Mr. Lambertson. He made a great show of studying them carefully, making Amanda turn her head this way and that.

"I'm no authority," he said at last, "but if you want my opinion, I prefer the second one."

The assistant smiled and gave a slight nod. It was her own favorite also.

"Very well then," he agreed. Then he turned to Amanda, who was reaching into her pocket for her birthday money. "Save your money, my dear. It's my pleasure to pay for it."

Before she took the money, the assistant opened one of the glass-fronted cabinets on the wall behind her.

"Here's something else you might want to see." She pulled out a lovely little muff, a little roll of pillow, open in the middle so you could slip your hands into it to warm them. "This would be a good little muff for an elegant young lady, don't you think?" she asked Mr. Lambertson. "It goes with the hat very nicely."

She held it up and turned it this way and that, to display its many graces. The muff was covered in white silk, like the hat. Instead of embroidery trim, however, it was covered all over with poufy rows of lacy white ribbon. There ribbons were stitched and gathered into little puffs

like snowy clouds, and there were matching bows for extra decoration.

"Nicely indeed," Mr. Lambertson agreed. "We'll take it also!" And as quick as a wink, the muff was in Amanda's hand, and she slipped her hands inside it.

She blinked back tears, overwhelmed by her feelings. He was so generous, so kind! And yet here she was, sneaking behind his back and deceiving him!

But then, said the little voice inside, hadn't he deceived her also? All these years, and they'd never told her they weren't really her parents, that she'd had some other mother and father. And a sister too! And why had they taken her alone and not taken her sister Amelia also?

chapter 9

Amanda's joy at finding she had a sister soon turned to worry instead. Where was Amelia now? She hadn't the least idea where she was, or how to find her. Somehow, she had to track her down, but how to go about it?

She had to go back to Williamsburg, she had to! She hadn't asked Mr. Waller nearly enough questions. Even if he didn't know where Amelia was now, he might know where she could go for more information. What about the church? Would they have records too? The churchwardens were the ones responsible for the care of orphans, according to what Gardener John had told her.

And what about Fredericksburg? Would there be records there? And surely there was more that Mr. Waller himself could remember. What did Amelia look like? Was she fair or dark, large or small? What was the color of her eyes, the color of her hair? And did he know her mother too, before she died? And what about her sailor father? Did his ship ever return? Had he ever come back to Williamsburg?

So she begged Mr. Lambertson to take her back to Williamsburg when her hat was ready. She wanted to see it right away, she said. She couldn't wait to wear it.

He agreed right away with a smile. When she asked for a favor, he almost always indulged her. Her hat wouldn't be ready for several days, however, and it was an agony of waiting.

To make it worse, Jane kept plaguing her worse than ever. How she ever found out what Amanda was up to, Amanda couldn't imagine. She hadn't told a soul, but Jane figured it out somehow. She must have second sight — she was a witch, she was truly!

Amanda was in the garden when Jane appeared, her apron full of shriveled carrots and frost-bitten cabbage. She must have told the cook she'd bring her vegetables from the winter garden, but Amanda was sure she'd been following her.

"You've been sneaking around the courthouse, haven't you?" Jane said slyly. "Looking for the father who never wanted you?"

"It's none of your business what I do," Amanda said haughtily. "You're just jealous, and I don't blame you. I'm going to have the most charming new hat you've ever seen."

Jane looked put out for a moment, seeing that she hadn't succeeded in upsetting her. She recovered quickly, however, and tried again.

"And does Mr. Lambertson know what you're up to?"

At this, Amanda couldn't help but look guilty.

"Aha!" Jane crowed triumphantly. "You haven't told him, have you? What would he think if he knew that his dear precious girl was a common little liar?"

It was so unfair! But what would her father think if she told him? It would be awful for Jane to tell Mr. Lambertson she was lying to him — and to be right! At least, sort of. She wasn't really lying, just not telling all of the truth, and she had a very good reason.

She wanted to tell him everything, really she did, but she was afraid he'd get the wrong idea of it. He might think that she cared for a father she hadn't seen in years more than she cared for him, who'd loved her and taken care of her. Worst of all, thinking of the time she ran away, he might think that she wanted to leave them.

So Amanda waited in a perfect turmoil of anxiety. Every time she saw him, she searched his face for some sign that Jane had told her tale. Then she'd sigh with relief when he seemed the same as ever.

She was lucky about that, at least. Jane hadn't said anything to Mr. Lambertson, but only because couldn't decided which of them would end up in greater trouble — Amanda, for whatever she was up to, or her own self, for telling on her.

At last, at long last, the waiting was over. The hat would be ready now, and together they went back to Williamsburg. They agreed to meet again at one o'clock, just as before, only this time they'd meet at the tavern.

Amanda went first to the milliner's of course. She really couldn't wait to see her hat. She just hoped it was really ready. It was, and she immediately put it on, and it was just as perfect as she'd imagined. Then she hurried back to the courthouse. The door was open, as before, but this time the court was in session. The room was crowded with all sorts of people — the lawyers, the litigants, the witnesses, and a various crowd of curious onlookers. At the very back of the room, the black-robed magistrates sat facing the crowd on an elevated platform. The sheriff was in his box and Mr. Waller was at his desk, in front of the magistrates, surveying the assembly.

Amanda turned away from the courthouse with a sigh. There was no point in waiting. She'd heard Mr. Lambertson say how the cases went on and on, since the court didn't meet very often.

But what to do? She had over an hour before she'd meet her father. She didn't feel like going back to the milliner's. She felt too restless to look at silks and patterned calicos. Maybe she should pass the time by walking around Williamsburg. It was a fine, sunny day and she so seldom got to town.

Aimlessly, she wandered down Duke of Gloucester Street toward the Capitol. Living on the plantation as she did, she rarely saw such a busy scene. There were carts, horse-drawn carriages, and all sorts of people — young and old, rich and poor, some on foot, some pushing their carts, some on horseback, some riding in carriages.

She passed three ladies in an open carriage, looking as elegant as anything. When they saw Amanda they smiled at her, and she curtsied back in return. How lovely they were! Would she ever look like that, when she was grown up? Or would she be one of the servant girls scurrying by on their errands, as Jane foretold?

She could have wandered up and down the street for hours, just looking at all the shop windows and all the people. She even saw Lord Dunmore, the Governor of the Colony of Virginia, riding by in his carriage. It had curtains on the windows, his crest on the doors in gold and blue, and it was drawn by a matching pair of wonderful chestnut-colored horses. A driver in sky-blue livery sat high in front and a footman in a matching outfit rode behind it.

She'd just about gotten to the Capitol, past the shops and taverns and houses, when a puppy ran out from between two houses. It was the cutest little thing, white with brown spots and long floppy ears. The puppy lay down and looked at her with big, sad eyes. Its coat was dirty and scruffy, and it was painfully thin. It seemed to be a homeless stray.

"The poor thing must be hungry!" thought Amanda, and she dug around in her pocket for a bit of ham and biscuit that she'd brought along for the ride back from town.

"Here you go, little puppy," she said softly, putting some of it down just before her on the sidewalk, "here's some food." The puppy was afraid to come much closer, but the smell of food was too much for it. After a little bit, it came timidly up to her, smelled the ham and biscuit, and then gobbled it up. The puppy licked up even the crumbs off the sidewalk, and then looked at her longingly, as if begging for more.

This time, she held a chunk in her hand and held it out to him carefully, hoping he wouldn't bite her fingers. He came right up to her and nibbled it gently, and then when it was gone he licked her hand. She reached down to pet it, but it trotted off down the street. She couldn't help but smile, the way it wiggled its tail with doggy delight and stopped every few feet to smell something. It kept stopping and looking back, as if it wanted her to follow it. So she did.

She followed the puppy a little way, but then out of the corner of her eye she thought she saw Mr. Waller. Maybe the court had taken a recess for dinner? She'd only had a glimpse so she wasn't sure, but it certainly seemed like that's who it was. Whoever it was,  though, she couldn't see him. He must have turned down another street at the corner.

If it was Mr. Waller, then this was her chance. Should she follow him? She hesitated for a moment or two and then hurried after off in the direction she thought he'd been going. When she turned the corner though, he wasn't there. The street wasn't very long, so he must have turned off at the footpath, there in the middle.

Yes, there he was! It was someone who looked like him from behind, anyway. The man had a long stride and he was going so much faster. She had to move very quickly if she hoped to catch him!

It was hard for her, in her stays and her nice silk dress with long, full petticoats, and her shoes with their little heels and leather shoes. It wasn't very long before she stumbled and fell, and when she got up again, she couldn't see Mr. Waller — or anyway the man she thought was him — not anywhere.

She'd lost him! She felt a wave of bitter disappointment. And then, looking around at her surroundings, she realized that she was lost as well. She didn't know Williamsburg very well, and she'd been concentrating so hard on keeping sight of the Mr. Waller, she hadn't paid any attention to where she was going.

She had to get back to the main part of town, but where was she exactly? There were hardly any buildings to be seen, just one large red brick building that looked grim and scary. It had a great wall around it and hardly any windows, and there weren't any people coming in or going out.

It must be the gaol, she thought. What else would have such a high brick wall and no windows? Could that be where Mr. Waller went? Did she dare to go there to ask for him?

As she stood there wondering what to do, she had the eeriest feeling that someone was watching her. She glanced quickly over her shoulder and saw that her feeling was right.

Just one brick building that looked grim and scary

There was a man not far away, just standing there and staring at her.

Where had he come from? Had he come from the gaol? Was he a prisoner, just released? Was he the gailor? Whoever he was, he had a very odd and frightening appearance. His suit had once been elegant and fine — the material must have been expensive. Now, however, it was stained and worn, and he was dressed very strangely. His waistcoat was buttoned all wrong, and one side hung down longer than the other. One knee of this britches was unbuckled and his jacket looked like he'd put it on in a hurry. If he'd had a different look on his face, she might have felt sorry for him. The way he was looking at her, however, was scary.

She walked a bit faster and then turned the next corner quickly. When she looked back, however, he was following her. He saw her looking back at him, and smiled at her. His smile wasn't nice at all. It gave her the shivers.

Too late, she realized that she'd gone in the wrong direction. She was heading away from the main part of town, instead of heading toward it. There weren't any other people around that she could see, except for the man who still was following her.

What should she do? She thought of screaming for help, but wouldn't she seem foolish? After all, what had he really done? And anyway who would hear her? From the way he was looking at her now, obviously amused by her fear, it might only encourage him.

So she kept on walking, her heart beating loudly. She didn't know where she was going any more. Her only thought was to get away, but no matter how hard she tried, the man kept getting closer and closer. Faster and faster she walked, and he too walked faster. Not too fast, just enough to slowly close the gap between them. It was a game to him, it seemed, and he was enjoying it.

Not far away was a great white building with a long front porch. A sign out front proclaimed it to be Christiana Campbell's Tavern. She was afraid to go inside — what a scandal it would be, for her to end up in a bar room! — so she turned onto the pathway that led to the back.

Behind the tavern was a large open courtyard with a scattering of smaller buildings. One must be the kitchen, she was sure — the one with smoke coming out of the chimney — and others looked to be a smokehouse and a dairy, and that little one to the side smelled like it must be a "necessary".

There wasn't another soul in sight at all — not him, not anyone. How could it be? Surely there must often be servants running back and forth all the time, at least between the tavern and the kitchen. Somehow she'd managed to miss them all. How could she be so unlucky?

It wouldn't have helped her anyway, she quickly realized. No servant would raise their hand against a gentleman. And despite his state of disarray, his clothes were the clothes of a gentleman.

She had to keep going, for he must surely be close behind her. Soon she found herself in a complicated maze of fences enclosing gardens, fields, and courtyards — white picket fences, split rail fences, some simply sticks nailed together or plain brown boards. One opened into the next with swinging gates, but some of them seemed to have no outlet. She was terrified that she'd find herself in one of those dead-end enclosures, with no way out — she had to get out of there quickly!

Finally she saw a gate that seemed to lead out onto a roadway. Hurrying, almost running, she made her way out to the street with relief. She took a moment catch her breath and look around her. The man wasn't in sight. At last she'd gotten ahead of him!

She had to find some place to hide. She couldn't go on running and running. She'd gotten a stone in her shoe and a sharp, piercing pain in her side, and she was nearly breathless.

She desperately looked up and down the street and then she saw it. Not too far away, at the corner of a fenced-in field, was a rough white wood building. It wasn't a house — it looked to be some sort of barn or stable. The two small windows that she could see didn't have any glass in them, but only slanted wooden slats across their openings, there was a tiny door high up on the corner wall, with no outside steps leading up to it. On the other side there were two large, barn-like doors on great iron hinges.

Ignoring the pain in her side, she ran as fast as she could to get there. Anxiously she tried the door on the

ℐt looked to be some sort of barn or stable

right. Yes, it was open! As she pulled it open further, the iron hinges made a terrible noise. Was the man close enough to hear it? She slipped inside and closed the door quickly behind her. She hoped the sound wasn't really as loud as it seemed to be.

After being so long outside in the bright sunlight, it took her a moment for her eyes to adjust to the dark inside the building. She stood there for a moment, breathing hard, wondering what she'd chosen as a refuge.

Finally her vision returned and she looked around. It was definitely a stable, she decided. There weren't any horses to be seen, but one side was partitioned into half-high enclosures. Leather tack and saddles were hanging on the wall and the dirt floor was littered with straw. Above was a loft full of bales of hay, boxes, and barrels.

A young girl, even younger than she was, was standing in the middle of the room sweeping the dirty old straw into little piles. She was barefoot, in a much-mended cotton bedgown and thin linen petticoat, without a cloak or any kind of woolen covering. She looked pale with cold, and no wonder. She wasn't wearing much at all, for an unheated building in the wintertime.

When she saw Amanda, she laid her broom against the wall and came over to her.

"Can I help you?"

In addition to looking cold, the girl looked awfully thin and weary. There were ugly bruises on her face and a white linen bandage covering part of her left arm. All the same, she seemed kind and friendly.

"A man is chasing me," Amanda told her hurriedly, "and I'm afraid. Can you hide me?"

The girl pointed to a rickety ladder leading up to the stable loft.

"Up there, quickly!" she whispered. "Hide yourself behind the bales of hay."

Amanda scampered up the ladder as quickly as she could, tucking her long skirts out of the way as best she was able. No sooner had she made a small wall of hay bales and crouched down behind it, when the doors burst open and her pursuer strode roughly into the stable.

"I'm looking for a runaway servant!" he lied boldly to the stable-girl, who'd meanwhile resumed her sweeping. "She's a young girl, about your age or a little older. Have you seen her? You'd better tell me! She's stolen her clothes and some gold besides."

With remarkable poise, the girl just kept on sweeping.

"There hasn't been anyone here, so you needn't be bothering me!" Amanda was amazed at how the girl had suddenly changed. What an actress she was! She sounded as mean as Jane ever did and she looked the very image of a surly servant.

She held out her hand and gazed at the man with greed in her eyes.

"What does she look like? If it's gold you're seeking, you can afford to pay. For a shilling I'll look out for her."

The man looked at her suspiciously and then peered around the room. Amanda held her breath and closed her eyes, but the girl just stood there, holding out her hand. He stared extra long at the ladder, as if he was going to climb up to look in the loft, but maybe the ladder seemed too rickety for him to try it. Instead he shrugged, scowled, and went back outside, slamming the door behind him.

Amanda started to rise and leave her hiding place, but the girl signaled her urgently to stay where she was.

Sure enough, an instant later the door opened and he stuck his head in once again. He looked around, but all he saw was the girl (now she was calmly sweeping again) and he left them.

The girl waited, sweeping away, for some time afterwards. Then she set down her broom and peeked out the door, looking carefully up and down the alley in both directions.

"I think he's gone," she said at last. "You can come out now."

Amanda got up then, stiff from her crouching behind the hay for so long, and made her way carefully down from the loft. She was covered in bits of hay and straw. It clung to her gown, to her hair, and everywhere. The stable girl smiled, and then started to laugh at how funny she looked, like a fine lady scarecrow. At first Amanda was hurt and offended, but after a moment she joined in laughing too.

"Here, let me help you." The stable girl started to brush the straw off Amanda's back, still laughing. "You've straw all over — your stockings, your hair, even your hat! It's a pretty hat, I must say. I've hardly seen one prettier." She sounded admiring and pleased for her, thought Amanda. Not full of envy like Jane.

"Would you like it?" Amanda quickly took off the hat and held it out to her. "After all, you saved me from that horrible man."

Embarrassed, the stable girl backed away.

"Oh no, I couldn't!" She reached out to stroke one of the silken ribbons, and then quickly withdrew her hand. "He wouldn't let me keep it, anyway."

"Who is 'he'?"

"My Master. My owner."

The Lambertsons had indentured servants, like Jane, and even slaves, but Amanda had never thought much about it. Now for the first time, she stopped to consider it. What did it mean, for one human being to 'own' another? She looked again at the bruise on the girl's face, large and yellow and purple. Did it mean you could beat them if it pleased you? And even if you treated them well, as the Lambertsons treated their servants, with plenty to eat and kind words, and only gentle reprimands, even when they deserved it — what was it like to be owned by another person?

"Is he mean to you?" Amanda said at last. "Your face is covered in bruises! And what is the matter with your arm?"

The girl looked at the bandage as if she'd forgotten all about it and only just remembered.

"Oh, nothing. Just a little burn, that's all. I fell onto some hot coals."

"Does he beat you that hard?" Amanda asked, horrified. "Did he knock you into the fire?"

The girl hesitated and looked away, before she answered.

"He says it's my fault." She sounded as if she almost believed it. "He says I'm stupid and clumsy. I don't think he means to be so bad. It's just that Mr. Pryor — that's his name — has such a temper when I do things wrong."

"Not Mr. Pryor!"

"Why, do you know him?" The girl looked dismayed. "I'm sorry if he's a friend of yours."

"Oh no," Amanda quickly replied. "I only saw him once, that's all."

"It's not so bad really," the girl continued, obviously relieved that she hadn't offended Amanda, "it's just that it was so much better before, in Fredericksburg."

Amanda's ears pricked up. The girl was from Fredericksburg! Maybe she knew something about her sister.

"I have a sister in Fredericksburg." She began eagerly but then she felt suddenly hesitant, just as she had at the Secretary's Office. What if Amelia was dead and buried, lying in her grave? If that was the case, did she really want to know about it? Wasn't it better to imagine her happy and alive, than to know the worst of things?

"A sister?" The girl looked at her curiously.

"So I'm told, anyway. I haven't seen her in years, and I don't really know her."

"What's her name? Maybe I've heard of her."

Amanda said a little prayer. Please God, let this girl know where my sister is. And let her be alive and happy.

"Her name's Amelia."

The girl's eyes widened.

"Why, that's my name! Amelia! Amelia Watkins."

Amanda couldn't say a word.

"They told me I had a sister," the girl went on, "the people who took me to Fredericksburg. They told me her name was Amanda. But it was so long ago, I hardly remember her."

She looked at Amanda with a strange mixture of hope and fear, as if she hardly dared to ask the question.

"Are you my sister?"

chapter 10

Looking back on that day, Amanda was forever enormously grateful. She was grateful for the court being in session, for people at the Secretary's Office going so early to dinner. She was even grateful for the terrible man who'd chased her. If it hadn't been for all these things, would she ever have found her sister?

At the time, however, she could only think, "Whatever can I say to Father?" He must have known about Amelia. He and Mrs. Lambertson had taken her home but they hadn't taken Amelia. They'd taken one and left the other behind.

No wonder they'd hidden it from her all these years that she ever had a sister! And now she'd found out the secret, and found her sister on her own. And she'd done it on the sly, Amanda realized guiltily. She had her own share of hiding things, hadn't she, lying and deceiving them about what she was doing?

So she didn't know what to say to Mr. Lambertson, and she didn't have much time to think about it. She only just had time to go back to the milliner's and retrieve her new hat before she had to meet him at the tavern.

She got to the tavern just in time and hurried into the dining room. She'd been running so much, her face was flushed and she was still out of breath, her gown was untidy, and her hair was coming unpinned and escaping from under her cap in wispy tendrils.

Mr. Lambertson gave her a look, as if to say "you're late!" Or maybe he was wondering what on earth she'd been up to. But he didn't voice his thoughts, whatever they were. He only told her to sit down, and then said her new hat was very becoming.

All through the meal, Amanda was absent-minded and distracted. Her chicken pie was very fine, but she hardly noticed what she was eating. She even turned down the apple pudding for dessert.

"No pudding?" Mr. Lambertson looked at her, surprised. "But it's your favorite! Are you ill? Is something wrong?"

Amanda hesitated. She was tempted to say yes, she wasn't feeling so well. Too much sun, perhaps. It would be explain her odd behavior. She wouldn't have to explain anything and she wouldn't risk his being upset. Seeing how he looked at her though, so concerned and caring, she felt she had to tell him the truth.

"I want to tell you, but I'm afraid you'll be angry with me."

He reached across the table and took her hand.

"My dear girl, what you could do that would make me angry, I can't imagine."

Amanda looked down at the table for a long, long while, summoning her courage. Then she took a deep breath and began.

"The other time we came here, I went to the courthouse."

"You talked to Mr. Waller, didn't you?"

"You know?"

"He mentioned it to me the last time I saw him. I was wondering when you would tell me."

Flustered by this news, Amanda paused to collect herself. She looked away, outside the window. The sky had turned grey and cloudy and it had begun to snow. She watched the large, lacy snowflakes, drifting slowly, gently down from the sky.

"Please don't be angry with me," she said softly. "I didn't want to upset you. I didn't want you to think I didn't love you just as much as before. It's just that when I found out — well, all those things about what happened, and I'd never known it — it was like I didn't even know myself, who I was or where I came from. I just had to find out more."

"It's all right, my dear. I'm not angry. I understand." He smiled to show he meant it. "And now would you like some pudding after all?"

Amanda looked at him, astonished and upset. But what about her sister? Why hadn't they taken her too? If he knew about the clerk and everything, why didn't he even try to explain?

"He said I had a sister." She couldn't help but sound like she was feeling, upset and even angry too. "A sister, a younger sister. Why did you take me and not her too?"

She looked at Mr. Lambertson searchingly, waiting for his explanation. How many times she'd tried to imagine this moment and what he might say! As she'd tried to picture it, he'd looked angry and sometimes he'd looked guilty. Sometimes he'd been evasive and sometimes he'd been sad. But now that it came to it, in reality, his reaction was something she'd never imagined. He only looked surprised

"A sister? You had a sister?"

"You didn't know?"

"We never had any idea!" He shook his head in astonishment. "If we'd known, do you think we would have separated you? Can you really think we're such monsters?"

At that she couldn't help but start to cry. The tears ran down her face, very few and very softly. He handed her his handkerchief, his best silk one from Paris, and she gently dried her eyes.

"I didn't know what to think." She kept the handkerchief in her hands, unconsciously twisting and untwisting it. She thought she might need it soon again. "How could I? It was all such a shock! Suddenly, nothing was what I thought it was."

He gave her a look full of sadness and pity.

"We'd planned to go to the court that day. But then your mother — Mrs. Lambertson — came down with a fever, so we didn't go. A friend of mine took care of everything as our agent. He went to the court and brought you home, but he never said anything about a sister. Mr. Waller never mentioned it either and I didn't think to ask him." He reached out and took her hand. "Dear Amanda, I'm so sorry. I promise you, we'll do everything in our power to find her."

Amanda felt as if a great weight had been lifted from her heart.

"You don't have to," she said softly. "I found her myself, just an hour ago."

chapter 11

After that day, Amanda thought the worst was behind her. Unfortunately, she was wrong.

Mr. Pryor didn't want to let Amelia go, not for kindness, not for money, not for anything. She was his, he said, and he wanted to keep her. Why he felt that way was a total mystery. You wouldn't have thought he cared if she lived or died, the way he treated her. And he could have bought two indentures to replace her, at least, for the money Mr. Lambertson offered him.

"We'll have to go to court," Mr. Lambertson said finally.

"It's going to be hard," his friend Mr. Wilkerson counseled. They were closeted together in Mr. Lambertson's study. Amanda was in the next door parlor, trying to listen through the wall. "Remember what happened with Penney."

"That was a different thing, altogether!" Mr. Lambertson sounded very sure of himself, but Mr. Wilkerson sounded pretty sure of himself too.

"You might even get into trouble over Amanda," Mr. Wilkerson warned him, "pretending she's your daughter. As I've told you before, her position is very irregular. It would be different if you'd adopted her, but you haven't."

Amanda was dying to hear what Mr. Lambertson said in reply, but just then Jane stuck her head in the doorway. She'd been eavesdropping too, through the door from the study to the hall.

"Just wait and see, you'll lose again!" she sneered. "Just like it was with Penney! Your sister's no better than she was. Take the word of a servant against the master? That'll be the day! And they'll take you too, I bet you! Just like Mr. Wilkerson told your father." She gave Amanda a nasty smirk and flounced off, laughing.

When the court day came, Mr. Lambertson went off to Williamsburg, while Amanda and Mrs. Lambertson waited anxiously at home. Amanda kept wandering in and out of Mr. Lambertson's study like a sleepwalker. She was in a daze — was she living a dream, or a nightmare?

Would Jane's words come true once again? Had she found her sister, only to lose the only mother and father she'd ever known?

When they heard Mr. Lambertson coming back from Williamsburg, Amanda and Mrs. Lambertson both rushed out to greet him. Seeing them, he shook his head.

"I don't know. They haven't decided."

Amanda could hardly restrain herself.

"How could they leave her with Mr. Pryor? How could they? He doesn't teach her any sort of skill, just sweeping and cleaning and scrubbing the floors. And whenever he pleases, he beats her! And he even pushed her into the fire!"

"He said he's teaching her how to be a good house-wife." Mr. Lambertson was still angry and his voice was tight. "And there's nothing wrong with beating a servant if they've done something wrong. He said she was just stupid and clumsy, and she fell in the fire by herself. It's all a question of who the magistrate chooses to believe."

"How could he believe a man like that?"

"He's a very good liar, I'm afraid. He was very convincing. And Amelia's just an apprentice, after all. "

The next afternoon, the sheriff came to the house just before dinner. He and Mr. Lambertson went into the study and closed the door. Amanda went into the parlor and put her ear against the wall. By now, she was very good at eavesdropping, and not the least bit guilty about it.

"The case is decided," she heard the sheriff say. He didn't sound happy. "I thought I should come and tell you in person. It's bad news, I'm afraid."

"We lost?"

"I'm afraid so, though I think the magistrate had a hard time deciding it. Decide it he did, however, and Mr. Pryor has won. Amelia stays where she is."

Amanda felt like she would faint dead away, right there in the parlor by the wall. Somehow she managed to creep up the stairs to her bedroom. Then she cried for a long, long time.

Somehow, she managed to get through dinner that day, pretending she hadn't overheard them. All through the meal, Mr. Lambertson looked angry, never meeting her eyes. Mrs. Lambertson didn't even come to the table. She sent Jane in to say that "she had a dreadful headache".

Neither Mr. Lambertson nor Amanda could eat much of anything, they just picked at their food in the terrible silence. Then he took her to his study, sat her down, and told her what the Sherriff had said.

"Isn't there anything else we can do?" Amanda pleaded. "Is that all there is?"

"I'm afraid it's over and done with." Mr. Lambertson sounded certain. "We'll just have to wait until she's eighteen and finishes her apprenticeship. Then she'll be free and independent."

"Oh no!" Amanda cried out in anguish. "Wait until she's eighteen? That would be forever! And in the meantime, who knows what he might do to her! The way he treats her, she might die before then!"

"I don't like it either," Mr. Lambertson said unhappily, "but we tried our best and we lost it. There's nothing more we can do"

Amanda couldn't think of anything more to say, but she couldn't stop thinking about it constantly and feeling miserable. She'd been so excited to find her sister at last, and now she'd lost her again — or as good as. The worst had come to past.

Or was it really the worst? Not if Jane was right again, and she'd been right about everything so far.

Jane knew it too, and lost no opportunity to remind her. Not in a way that Amanda could complain about it; not so that anyone could overhear. Oh no, Jane was too clever for that. Whenever the Lambertsons were around, she was the very model of a perfect servant. It was "yes Miss," and "no Miss," and "as you please, Miss," and butter wouldn't melt in her mouth, the way she said it.

When she and Amanda were alone, however, she'd torment her as much as she could.

"Just you wait, Miss Amanda," she'd whisper, when no one else could hear her, "this is only the beginning. Next they'll be coming for you, to take you away from here and give you a proper apprenticeship, to learn something better than fancy needlework and French. It'd be different if the Lambertsons adopted you as their own, but they haven't, have they? They don't really see you as their daughter, for all they pretend that they do."

Amelia tried not to let it show, but Jane's words continued to haunt her. Why did Jane ever have to come to work for them?! Things were all so much simpler, before. Now she'd learned the truth and it had only made her miserable and unhappy. Were even worse things yet to come?

If the magistrate believed Mr. Pryor's lies, who knew what could happen? Everything else Jane had said had turned out to be true. Would she be right again?

chapter 12

Of all the things that Jane ever said, what she said about the Lambertsons not really wanting her was the worst thing ever. They should have adopted her, and they hadn't. Hadn't Mr. Wilkerson had said it too? Why hadn't they done it? Was it because they didn't really love her, as Jane insisted? Would they send her away when her indenture was over, when she turned eighteen?

She was afraid to ask Mr. or Mrs. Lambertson about it. What if she did and they said they didn't love her that much, to actually adopt her? What if they said something that sounded nice but she could tell they were lying? If the truth was as bad as Jane had told her, did she really want to know?

She couldn't stop thinking about it all the same. Why hadn't they adopted her? She tried to imagine the possible reasons, but none of them were good. Why didn't they adopt her and Amelia too? The solution was so simple and yet they wouldn't do it.

Thinking of Amelia, she figured out how to ask the question. She could ask about adopting Amelia and not ask about herself. She waited to choose the right moment, when she and Mr. Lambertson were together alone.

"What if Amelia had parents who could take care of her, would that help?" Amanda tried to make it sound like a casual question. "Would they be able to get her away from Mr. Pryor?"

"Of course it would," Mr. Lambertson agreed. "That's why she was apprenticed to begin with. But you know she doesn't have parents like that — just your father, and he's always away at sea."

Amanda turned to him then, her face full of hope.

"Couldn't you and Mrs. Lambertson adopt her?" She held her breath to hear the answer.

Mr. Lambertson studied her face and he seemed to understand what she was really asking.

"You can't adopt a child who has parents," he explained to her, "unless the parents agree to it. Don't you think we would have adopted you long ago, if we could have done it? Your father would have to agree and we don't know where to find him. He might come back and ask for you back again. He's still alive, as far as we know."

"Oh." Now that at last she knew the answer, Amanda felt strangely torn. She wanted so much for the Lambertsons to adopt her, for them to be her parents forever and for real. But then again, she had a sailor father out there somewhere. She had a tie to him too, a tie that could never be broken. He'd had to leave her, but he'd loved her too. That's what Mr. Waller told her.

One morning, not too much later, an old woman showed up. She was dressed all in black and her face was full of wrinkles. She had a look, like she was looking right on through you, and she seemed as old as time itself.

She stood there at the door, with an old black horse tied up to the fence post — a horse so laden down with bags and bundles that there was no room left to sit on it, to ride. She'd come from France, she said, and she was making her way to her family in Richmond. She begged a bit of food, for pity's sake, and she'd tell your fortune in return.

Mrs. Lambertson wanted to send her away, but Amanda begged her not to. The old woman did look hungry, after all, and Amanda wanted to hear her fortune. Mrs. Lambertson thought it was all nonsense, telling fortunes, but Amanda wasn't so sure. What about her Twelfth Night fortune? She'd gotten a ship, and her father was a sailor. That was only a silly game, not even a proper fortune, but that had been right.

Amanda begged so hard to let the old woman tell her fortune that Mrs. Lambertson finally agreed. She wasn't very happy about it though. What if this so-called fortune was a bad one? Amanda was in such poor spirits as it was. So she slipped five pence into the old woman's palm as she led her into the parlor.

"Whatever you do, don't upset her," she whispered. "I'll give you double that if the fortune's good."

The old woman gave her a long, steady look, whether for good or for ill was uncertain.

"It's the cards themselves that decide," she said at last. "I only read what they say."

They all sat down at the little gaming table, one on each side. Amanda sat to the left of the old woman and Mrs. Lambertson sat across. The old woman took out the cards — they were wrapped in a blue silk handkerchief — and shuffled them. Then she held the deck out to Amanda, face down, and fanned them out.

"Pick a card and turn it over."

Amanda dutifully picked out a card and turned it over. It was a picture of two children standing in front of a wall, with a great yellow sun shining in the sky above them.

"Le Soleil," the old woman said, and Amanda nodded. Thanks to her French lessons, she understood. "Le soleil" meant "the sun."

The old woman pointed to one of the children on the card. "That is you. And the other —"

"That's my sister!" Amanda cried. "Is the fortune about my sister?"

Mrs. Lambertson started to intervene but the old woman held up a hand to stop her.

"Perhaps, perhaps not," the woman said, and she laid down four more cards on the table. She put one above the Sun card that was Amanda. She laid one card below the Sun card and one on either side of it. Then she silently studied them.

The card below Amanda's card had many golden goblets. Amanda counted them one by one. There were ten of them. The card above her was a man in a cloak holding up a lantern. The one to the left was a single sword with flames all around it, and the one to the right was a lady pouring water out of two pitchers, with eight stars in the sky above her.

"You've been separated from someone," the old woman said, pointing at the sword, and then she pointed at the man with the lantern. "You're looking for to find him."

"My father! What does it say?" Amanda leaned forward in excitement. "Do I find him?"

The woman pointed to the lady with the stars.

"You will succeed in the end, if you persevere and are lucky."

Amanda was overjoyed, and Mrs. Lambertson was distressed to see how excited she was.

"Remember, Amanda, it's only a game of cards. You shouldn't get your hopes up."

"Is not a game." The old woman sounded like she was offended. "The cards, they don't lie. Not to believe is foolish."

"But what do I do?" Amanda asked eagerly. "How do I find him?"

"There is water. Waters. Many waters." The woman pointed again at the car with the stars. "You see — the woman is pouring her waters into the ocean."

Amanda reached to pick up the card and the old woman reached out as if to stop her. Then she seemed to change her mind, and let her.  Amanda held the card up close to her face and studied it closely. She tried to memorize every detail, to think about it later.

The woman on the card was kneeling by a body of water. Only part of it was on the card, so you couldn't tell the size of it. The old woman said it was the ocean, but it could just as well have been a lake or a pond, or maybe even a river. Whatever it was, the kneeling woman was pouring even more water into it out of her two pitchers. Amanda thought they must be magic pitchers, for there seemed to be no end to the water. It looked like she could go on pouring and pouring out water forever and the pitchers would never run out of it.

"Yes, water," Amanda repeated. "He's a sailor, you see." Then she sighed with disappointment. She'd had such hopes, after the way the fortune-telling started. Her sister, her sailor father, their being separated — the old woman seemed to know everything. But it was all things she already knew, and nothing to help her.

"I already knew he was a sailor," she said at last, "but how do I find him? Do the cards tell you that?" She looked at the old woman anxiously.

The woman stared at the cards a very long time, as if willing them to tell her. Then she shook her head and pointed at the man with the lantern, the card that lay above Amanda's card. "It is you who must find the answer. The cards will tell no more."

chapter 13

Mrs. Lambertson gave the old woman some bread and leftover ham, and then sent her off to Richmond. Amanda watched her walk away, leaning on her stick and leading the heavily-laden horse behind her.

The old lady's fortune left Amanda feeling strangely troubled. There was the part about her sister, and being separated from her sailor father — it all seemed so right at first. And then, to say that she'd succeed in the end (but only if she was lucky?) and not to tell her how to do it! And the lady with all the water — that was supposed to be the solution, but what did it all mean? Or was it only a game, like her mother said? Did it really mean anything at all?

The rest of the day, and all the day after, Amanda thought of almost nothing else. She was too restless to sew, too absorbed in thinking about the puzzle to read or study. She wanted to go for a long, long walk, but it was raining pretty hard. So, restless and distracted, she wandered here about the house.

Mrs. Lambertson was sitting in the parlor trying to sew and Amanda was driving her crazy.

"You must sit down, Amanda!" she said at last. "You will make me quite mad if you go on this way."

She got out a book and thrust it into Amanda's hands. "Here, why don't you read a story? Maybe it will distract you."

Amanda dutifully sat down and opened the book, but she couldn't pay attention to it. As soon as she'd read a word or two, she'd immediately forget it. She might as well have been asleep and turning the pages blindly. She put down the book and picked up her needlework. That was even worse than trying to read — her stitches were all wrong and she kept pricking her finger with the needle. So she tried just sitting there, looking out the window. Outside it was raining steadily.

It worked for a while, but she couldn't sit still for long. Soon enough, she started fidgeting. Then, unconsciously,

Mrs. Lambertson was trying to sew

she started tapping on her foot on the floor. Tap, tap. Tap, tap. Tap, tap, tap. Tap, tap. Tap. In time to the rain drops.

"You must stop, Amanda!"

"I'm sorry, Mother! I'm so nervous, I can't help it!"

"You simply must calm down!" Mrs. Lambertson was anxious herself, but for a different reason. She was mad at herself for ever giving in, for letting that old woman tell Amanda's fortune. It was just foolishness, she was sure — and now Amanda was worse than ever.

She picked up the Virginia Gazette from the table and handed it over to Amanda. "If a book is too much for you, dear, why not try the newspaper? If that doesn't work, you'll have to go outside. Whether it's raining or not, I simply can't stand it."

Amanda took the newspaper and obediently tried to read again, but it wasn't any better. Her eyes kept skipping over the page, seeing only words here and there, without any sense to them.

Then, on the second page, her eye was drawn to headline. It was in large, bold type and the words leapt out — "The Ship WATTERS."

"That's it!" She cried happily.

Mrs. Lambertson looked up sharply.

"Whatever are you talking about?"

"Water! That's what it means!"

Amanda handed the paper to Mrs. Lambertson, pointing to the little notice.

"The Ship WATTERS," it said, "Lying at NORFOLK, will take in TOBACCO, on Liberty of Consignment. At

Eight Pounds a Ton. Apply to the Master on Board, or to the Subscriber in Fredericksburg."

Mrs. Lambertson read it and then looked at Amanda, clearly puzzled.

"What are you talking about, my dear? It's just an advertisement that this ship is offering to take people's tobacco for them."

"It's the name of the ship," Amanda explained. "The name of the ship is 'The Watters'. That's it, don't you see? The answer to the puzzle. That's what it meant, the lady with the stars. And the ship is in Norfolk!"

Mrs. Lambertson thought this was pretty silly, and Mr. Lambertson thought it was pure foolishness.

"An old lady with a pack of cards, and now see what we've gotten ourselves into!" he told Mrs. Lambertson. "Why did you ever let her in? Why did you let her tell Amanda's so-called fortune?"

"I know, I know," Mrs. Lambertson agreed unhappily. "I didn't want to, I really didn't. But Amanda was so keen to hear her fortune that I gave in to her. And I thought she'd just make up something nice, to make us happy. I even promised her money if she did. I never imagined it would all be so serious!"

The damage was done, however much they regretted it. Amanda couldn't rest. She was sure her sailor father was on that ship, The Watters.

Eventually Mr. Lambertson had no choice but to give in. He knew that Amanda would never rest easy — nor would he! — if he didn't. He held out for one entire day, but he was worn down by the end of it.

"All right," he said wearily. "Tomorrow I'll go to Norfolk."

chapter 14

Amanda hardly slept all night and she was the first one up in the morning. Mr. Lambertson went off for Norfolk just after breakfast. It was nearly fifty miles, too much for a day's journey. If he was lucky and nothing went wrong, he might be back tomorrow. More likely, it would be even later.

Amanda made it through the first two days with increasing impatience. By the third day, she could hardly stand the thought of any more waiting.

"Go for a walk," Mrs. Lambertson told Amanda after they'd finished breakfast. She didn't want to go through another day like the day before, with Amanda pacing around and fidgeting. "Go for a long walk, or a ride. You're old enough now, you can ride one of the horses over to visit one of the neighbors. And when you come back, you can go help John in the garden. I'm sure he could use help, weeding and planting the beans. I don't want to see you at all today, except at mealtime."

Amanda didn't feel like visiting, so she just went out and rode around the fields and through the forest. It was a lovely day for riding, sunny and spring-like. It took her mind off things for a while.

Then she helped John in the garden. He made a row of evenly-spaced holes in the ground and she followed along behind him, dropping one bean in each of the holes. Then he smoothed the whole thing over, so the dirt covered the seeds. Later he would set up poles and trellises for the beans to climb.

It was calm and soothing there in the garden, with the bright sun shining down on the warm earth, surrounded by the tiny seedlings of the early vegetables like carrots and peas, and the dogwood trees covered with snow-white blossoms. It would have been a fine day, all in all, if it hadn't been for running into Jane, and Jane back to her old tricks of tormenting her.

Jane hadn't troubled her for the last several days. Not since they lost the court case to bring Amelia home. Amanda thought maybe now she was as miserable as could be, Jane would be satisfied and leave her alone. But

Jane would never be satisfied. She was just waiting for a good opportunity.

Amanda had managed to while away the day, what with riding around and helping in the garden. Now the sun was getting low in the sky and it was getting cold there in the garden.

"Enough of that," John said, patting down a last row of earth over the tiny seeds. "It's finished. Now go inside and warm yourself up. If you get a chill, your mother won't thank me."

Amanda was glad to follow his instructions. She stood up, brushed the dirt off her hands, and started up the pathway.

Jane was waiting for her, just by the kitchen doorway, eating an apple and laughing.

"I'm glad I'm not you," Jane greeted her. "I'm glad I'm not such a silly little girl as you are, with your head so full of foolish fancies."

Amanda knew she should just ignore her, but she just couldn't do it.

"I'd rather be me any day, than be like you," she snapped back. "You're the meanest, nastiest girl I ever heard of."

Jane wasn't upset at all. She just snickered. "You're just afraid of me and what I'll say, and I know it! Because I've been right all along about everything, haven't I been? A ship called Watters—I never heard anything sillier! I can't wait to be right again, and see how you look when Mr. Lambertson comes home empty handed."

"I'm not wrong, you'll see!" Amanda stamped her foot, overcome with anger. If only she could think of some clever response, something that would put Jane in her place for good and ever! But she never knew what to say—Jane always got the best of her.

Jane laughed and took another bite of her apple.

"That will be the day! Well I wouldn't hold my breath waiting for it. Your real father's probably dead, is what I think. Maybe he washed overboard!" And with that, she

threw the apple core away and went back into the kitchen.

It wasn't a very good night. Amanda had never had so much trouble sleeping. And when she did, Jane was even in her dreams, grinning her evil grin and making fun of her. The next day was little better. If anything, it was worse. Gone was the spring-like weather, the sunshine. Today was rainy, windy, and cold. Mrs. Lambertson looked out the window and sighed. A whole day cooped up with Amanda! And truth be told, she was feeling pretty anxious herself. Was it possible she was right, that they really might find her sailor father? And what about adoption — would he agree? It was too much to hope for.

All day long, Amanda busied herself with her needlework. She was making a pocket for Amelia. It was fine white linen, sturdy and strong, and she'd traced on it a beautiful design of vines and flowers. Her needlework was very nice and the design was beginning to take shape, with neat little chains and knots and satin stitches of hand-died wool threads in jewel-like colors. Every few minutes, though, she'd get up to look out the window, to see if Mr. Lambertson was coming yet.

Waiting and watching in a fever pitch of anxiety, with no distractions at all, was entirely exhausting. She finally fell asleep in her chair, just as the sun was setting. Of course that would be just when Mr. Lambertson finally came back from Norfolk.

"Amanda?" he called out as soon as he opened the front door. "Amanda? Where are you?"

She woke with a start, jumped out, and ran out to the hallway. There was Mr. Lambertson, as happy as could be, standing in the doorway. He took a few steps inside and Amanda could see a strange, yet somehow familiar-looking man, standing outside just a few steps behind him.

"Come here Amanda," Mr. Lambertson said gently. "Come and meet your father."

Mr. Watkins, her sailor father home at last, walked slowly up the step and over the landing. He just stood there, just inside the door, holding his cap in his hands and looking nervous.

For a long time they just stood there, not meeting each other's eyes. Then they both looked up and stared at each other for quite a long time without saying a word. What could they possibly say to each other?

It had been so very long. The last time they'd seen each other, Amanda didn't even remember it. After a while — it seemed like hours — Amanda took a hesitant step forward. Then he did too, and slowly, step by step, they came closer and closer together.

He reached out his weather-beaten hand to stroke her cheek, and she took his hand in hers and held it to her. Then he took her in his great, sun-browned arms, and held her tightly.

Not a word was said, nor was any word necessary.

Finally he looked up and spoke to Mr. Lambertson.

Amanda could see a strange
yet familar-looking man

"She's grown up so lovely. I guess I have you to thank for it." Then he noticed Mrs. Lambertson, standing there in the parlor doorway. "And your wife too. My little Amanda's a fine little lady."

Mrs. Lambertson had such a sad look in her eyes that Amanda couldn't stand it. She went over to her and took her hand, and drew her into the hallway.

"This is my mother," she said, and then she looked at Mr. Lambertson. "And my father too. Now I have two fathers. And a sister."

"Amelia!" Amanda's father seemed overcome. "Where is she?"

"Not here, not yet." Mr. Lambertson replied. "We'll explain it all over supper."

And explain it they did, about Mr. Pryor and the lawsuit, and all the while Mr. Watkins was silent, taking it all in and thinking.

"I'm a sailor and I live by the sea," he said at last when Mr. Lambertson was done talking and explaining. "I love the girls like my life itself, but that's the only life I know and I'm too old to change it."

He looked at Mr. and Mrs. Lambertson and his face was full of sadness but also resolution. It was as if he'd made a very hard decision, and it hurt, but he'd made it anyway.

"You said as how you love Amanda too — 'like your own daughter'. That's it, isn't it? And you've given her a good life, and all the things I can't give her. But what about poor Amelia?"

"We want her too," Mrs. Lambertson said quickly, "if only we could do it! But Mr. Pryor won't let her go. Our only chance is to adopt her."

Mr. Watkins turned to Amanda and took her hand across the table.

"Would you like to stay here?"

"Forever and ever!" she answered softly.

He looked sad to hear her answer, but also understanding. Then he turned back to Mr. and Mrs. Lambertson.

"Would you adopt them both, if you could? Amanda and Amelia?" His voice was rough but firm, like it was hard for him to ask the question, but he meant it.

Not even pausing to look at her husband, Mrs. Lambertson answered right away. "We would! If only ...."

"If only I'd agree, you mean? It would be the best life for them, there's no question." He paused, and no one dared to say anything. "But if I agreed," he went on, "then what would happen? Could I write them, from time to time? When I came back to land, could I see them?"

Mr. and Mrs. Lambertson both exclaimed at once, almost simultaneously.

"Of course you could!"

"You're their father!"

And so it was arranged, and everyone was satisfied.

Jane had been listening in, needless to say. Amelia knew she would be, and went looking for her afterwards.

"So I'm a silly girl, am I?" Amanda smiled in triumph. "Well, maybe this is a lesson to you! If I hadn't believed and hoped and kept trying, none of this ever would have happened."

For once, Jane had nothing to say, and that wasn't the end of it. Amanda finally had the courage to tell Mrs. Lambertson all the things that Jane had said and done, and Mrs. Lambertson gave her quite a talking to.

"She won't bother you anymore," Mrs. Lambertson told Amanda the next day. "Very soon, Jane will be leaving us." She didn't say where Jane was going, but it couldn't have been anywhere half as nice as the Lambertson's.

It wasn't very long, when the court was in session again, that Amanda and Amelia were adopted. It was a very different experience from before. This time, the magistrates were happy to agree with their case immediately.

Mr. Pryor's look was dark as murder when he heard the magistrate's decision. He stalked out of the courtroom like the Devil on fire, but there was nothing he could do about it. Anyone could see it was the best of all things for Amanda and Amelia, to say nothing of Mr. and Mrs. Lambertson.

They all rode home together afterwards in the Lambertson's carriage, Mr. and Mrs. Lambertson, Amanda and Amelia. Spring had come a last. Gone was the frost and snow, the bitter cold, the seemingly endless winter. The apple trees were in bloom, perfuming the air with the scent of springtime.

"This is the best day of my life!" Amelia said shyly. "I'm so happy, I could cry."

"Me too!" Amanda echoed joyfully, and she hugged them each in turn — first Mrs. Lambertson, and then Mr. Lambertson, and then Amelia, the longest of anyone.

"Now we're all together, and no one will ever be able to separate us. I feel like all this time I was living a dream, and now that I've woken up, it's even better than I ever could have imagined."

The carriage rolled along at a leisurely pace, with all of them smiling and happy. And trotting along behind, all the way home, was the little white and brown puppy.

The End

acknowledgments

The author would like to gratefully acknowledge Emma Hogan and the other models for the illustrations, Gunston Hall (home of George Mason) for its gracious assistance and wonderful house and grounds, Colonial Williamsburg for creating rich and enticing glimpses of the eighteenth century, Claude Moore Farm for the splendid fantasy of its Market Fairs, Cindy Palmer for her imaginative and useful suggestions, Stephanie Anderson and David Kosar for assistance with design and illustrations, and (last but not least) my dear husband Ted Borek for putting up with me all this time.